# The Green Family:  Brandon's Tree

## Also by Kevin Elkington

*Sixth Grade and Growing Up*

*Green Family:  New Home*

*Seventh Grade and Friendship*

*The Green Family:  Grateful*

*Eighth Grade and Togetherness*

*The Green Family:  Blessings*

*The Hsu Family:  Finding Happiness*

*The Green Family:  Bailey Being Bailey*

*The Hsu Family:  Calvin and Pedro, Good Friends*

# The Green Family:  Brandon's Tree

## By

## Kevin Elkington

For my loving parents, who inspired me to write books.

This is a work of fiction. Names, characters, places, and incidents either are the product of the author's imagination or are used fictitiously. Any resemblance to actual persons, living or dead, events, or locales is entirely coincidental.

ISBN: 9781797505794

Thank you very much for reading this book.

Greetings from Springdale, Minnesota.


Have a Hoot-Ha-Day!

I hope you enjoy reading this short-story book.

# Table of Contents

# Chapter 1

## More Blessed to Give

Believe it!

One day, Brandon was in his room and was looking out the window from his bedroom. He happened to see his father, John Green, standing on the front porch of the house, holding a coffee mug, and Brandon noticed that his father was in deep thought. Brandon rushed down to the front porch of the house to greet his father.

Brandon told his Dad, "Hi Dad!"

John Green replied, "Well good morning or should I say good mid-morning to you, Brandon."

Brandon replied, "I think good afternoon would be sufficient - don't you think, Dad."

John Green said, "Indeed – so it is - good afternoon."

Brandon was thinking to himself about how his father, John Green, used to be general counsel for Goldman Sachs Bank in New York City, New York.

Now, John Green is the proud owner of the hardware store and supermarket in the town of Springdale, Minnesota.

One day, my Dad told us: we are moving to the country, we will stick together as a family, and Bailey's life is more important than our Green family's maintenance of our privileged lifestyle.

We up-rooted to this little country town called Springdale, Minnesota. Believe it or not, it brought our entire family atmosphere together to be more peaceful and tranquil in our daily lives.

John Green was looking at Brandon, "Hello, Brandon, come to the earth."

Brandon said, "Yes, hi Dad."

John Green was looking and admiring the view which overlooks magnanimous, majestic, beautiful Lake Swan and the bountiful green marsh. He said, "Isn't this a beautiful setting?"

As Brandon and his father were sitting on the front porch of their arts and crafts style house and admiring the beautiful view, John Green told Brandon, "I have always striven for more and more success. Through Bailey, my outlook changed. I had a different outlook on life - it was not on the top of my list to move to this little town called Springdale, Minnesota."

As John Green continued to talk, he was looking at Brandon, "Brandon, sometimes timing is everything. Did you know that by sheer faith I happened to be in Wayzata, Minnesota, doing some legal work for my old friend who was ill?"

John Green continued, "I happened to encounter this elderly gentleman who was visibly very angry and upset and disappointed that his hardware store, which he thought he had sold, was un-sold. On a whim, I made a decision to buy Owen Farrell's hardware store because I felt sympathy for the elderly gentleman who was in such distress."

The journey the next morning involved me driving up to this town called Springdale, which is located about 120 miles north of Wayzata, Minnesota, to take a look at the hardware store which I bought on a whim. As I was driving, I began to think out loud, "Okay, sometimes things happen for some unknown reason. Life gives you a different outlook and does not give you a second chance. I thought it was an ideal town for us as a family to uproot here in Springdale, Minnesota. Here we are in Springdale, a quiet, picturesque, little, rural town, full of quietness, on the beautiful and tranquil Lake Swan. Now we have been living here for several years, I never thought I would do this - give up my prestigious job that I had to live in a small, rural, country town. Let alone, I never thought about owning a hardware store or a grocery market in a small, rural town in my life!"

Brandon replied, "You know what, Dad, I am very glad that you happened to be in Wayzata doing a favor for your old friend. I guess it was meant to be."

John Green replied, "Yes, indeed. I am over the moon, happy. I really appreciate doing the things that I would never have thought I would be doing. It is good to be blessed from giving."

Brandon replied, "Yes, one is blessed to give to people who need help, like Grandma Ruth always says."

John Green said, "You should believe in your heart; God is aware of everything that you are going through, good or bad. God knows everything and God sees everything."

Brandon replied, "Yes, God does know everything."

John Green said, "Although there are times and moments in your life that it seems, and appears, as if God does not care, God truly knows and is testing our patience."

Then Brandon chimes in, "Yes, Dad, Bailey sometimes really does try my patience, but by following God I still love him because he is my little brother."

John Green, "I know you really take care of your little brother. Thank you for taking care of your brother – you are looking out for him."

John Green continues to say, "Even though it seems as if God's time is taking a long time, let us remember that, in the end, God always comes through in every situation you encounter in life. Naturally, most of us are very impatient and do not like to wait for anything."

Brandon said, "Yes, we are always in a hurry – like we used to be in a hurry in New York sometimes."

John Green replied, "Most of the time, our expectations are not what they seem, and often times are dampened by things that are completely out-of-our-control. We are often looking back and reflecting or forced to look at things or spend time on what it might have been."

Brandon said, "Our confidence and our belief in having faith are always with us."

John Green replied, "Yes, in the end, everything will work out - the peace and contentment comes from focusing our thoughts."

Brandon replied, "Indeed, peace and contentment are very important things in everyone's life."

John Green replied, "You know, Brandon, when your younger brother was born with Down syndrome, our life was changed and also our way of thinking as well. We, the Green family, always know that the right thing you do is you grab it with both hands and take care of your family."

John Green continued, "In life, you only get one chance. We are doing the things I never thought we could do - yes, we took a lot of chances and had courage to up-root our family to this little town called Springdale, Minnesota."

More blessed to give.

By the way, as Brandon always says, and you guessed, it snows a lot in Springdale, Minnesota.

# Chapter 2

## Bailey's Trouble

Oh boy!

Oh boy!  Oh boy!

Oh boy!  Oh boy!  Oh boy!

Oh boy, oh boy, oh boy, oh boy, oh boy!

Where is that darn thing ------

Where did I put that darn thing!

Why can't I find it, that darn thing!

I'm in for big trouble.

Please, please, please, I really need to find that darn thing.

I just wish I knew what I did……

I did not take that darn thing!

Okay Bailey, you need to think!

Bailey, put your thinking cap on!

Okay Bailey, you really need to think hard!

Think, think, think!

Okay Bailey, put your thinking caps on and try to think hard, I mean really really hard.

I really need to find that darn thing.

Did I take it to school?

Did I take it when I was going for a walk?

Did I take it while bike riding?

Okay, Bailey, you really have to find that darn thing before Dad finds out it is missing!

I need help from Brandon because I know Brandon is a smart guy and he will help me find it.

I know Brandon will help me because Brandon is my big brother and Brandon always cares for me.

After all, I'm pretty sure Brandon would not like to see me get in trouble from Dad, would he?

Okay, I need to find Brandon……

Bailey was running towards Brandon's room that is upstairs from the kitchen. "Brandon, Brandon, Brandon," said Bailey as Bailey was knocking on Brandon's door and opening it with short breaths from running.

"Brandon, can you please help me find that darn thing?"

Brandon was telling Bailey to calm down and asked Bailey, "What darn thing?"

Bailey says, "Oh yeah, you don't know what the darn thing is, do you?"

Brandon replies, "No, I don't know what that darn thing is."

Bailey was looking at Brandon's face and was sitting on his bed.

"Oh, Brandon, I'm in for big, big, big trouble from Dad."

Brandon asks, "What kind of trouble Bailey?"

Bailey replies, "I know you have real wisdom - you can help me find that darn thing!"

By now, Brandon was getting a little exasperated, "Bailey, I don't understand what you mean! Look, Bailey, would you please, please, please tell me, what is this business about that darn thing - why are you in trouble with Dad? What trouble?"

Bailey starts to tell Brandon the story, "Don't you remember last week Dad showed you and me the old antique pocket watch that Dad was so proud of?

Anyway, I thought I would take it to Mr. Applebee and show it to him. However, I got a little side tracked. Instead, I went for a walk toward the marsh, near Lake Swan. I lost the watch! Now I don't know what happened!"

Brandon replies, "Oh no, Bailey!"

Bailey replies, "Yeah I know, oh boy is correct. What do you think we should do?"

Brandon responds, "We, what we?"

Bailey says, "Yeah we – you and me."

Brandon replies, "Oh no, I have nothing to do with this lost darn thing business. No way, no how."

Brandon continues, "Oh, Bailey, Bailey, Bailey, you are in for trouble."

Bailey responds by saying, "Brandon, you've got to help me find this thing, the darn thing, before Dad finds that it is not inside his desk drawer. If it's not there, I'm toast!"

Brandon tells Bailey, "Okay, Bailey, I'll help you with regards to this darn thing you are so desperately looking for. Oh Bailey, you truly are a HAM of a little brother."

Brandon continues, "Besides whatever this darn thing is, don't worry, we will find it together, okay!"

"You think so, Brandon, you really think we will find the watch?" said Bailey as he had a distressed look on his face looking at Brandon.

"Bailey, I most definitely will help you," said Brandon as he was watching Bailey's happy face emerge after Bailey heard the remark.

Bailey gave a big bear hug to Brandon, "Oh thank you, Brandon, you really are a kind-hearted, awesome cool big brother to me."

"You're welcome Bailey," as Brandon was showing Bailey the antique watch which Brandon had found near the marsh yesterday. Brandon enjoyed teasing his brother Bailey - what are big brothers for, anyway?

# Chapter 3

## Dinner with Teacher

Mrs. Judy Cohen is coming to dinner at our house.

Why?

She is Bailey's former math teacher.

Yes, that teacher, the teacher of the one and only math classroom, where Bailey created a major big drama………………!

Yes, that teacher, the teacher of the one and only math classroom, where Bailey just sort-of-lost his cool……………………..!

Yes, that teacher, the teacher of the one and only math classroom, where Bailey just tried to ignore it and lost his………………!

Yes, that teacher, the teacher of the one and only math classroom, where Bailey wasn't going to be whiny and lost his..............!

Yes, that teacher, the teacher of the one and only math classroom, where Bailey was not going to be wimpy and lost his.........!

Yes, that teacher, the teacher of the one and only math classroom, where Bailey was not going to be self-pitying and lost his......!

Yes, that teacher, the teacher of the one and only math classroom, where Bailey was not going to be impetuous by responding and lost his.........!

Yes, that teacher, the teacher of the one and only math classroom, where Bailey was not going to be brash and lost his.........!

Yes, that teacher, the teacher of the one and only math classroom, where Bailey was not going to be naïve and lost his............!

Yes, that teacher, the teacher of the one and only math classroom, where Bailey was not going to be throwing his final punches to Zach and Adam and Bailey lost his............!

Yes, that teacher, the teacher of the one and only math classroom, where Bailey was not going to be brash and lost his cool, somehow giving Zach and Adam a beauty.

Yes, that teacher, the teacher of the one and only math classroom, where Bailey was not going to be wimpy, whiny, and self-pitying because Bailey has Down syndrome.

He really, really, really tried to ignore it and was not to be impetuous, brash, or naïve. But, but, but, but, but, but…….!

Bailey just lost his cool and created a major big, big, big, big, big, big drama in Mrs. Cohen's class during math quiz time. Bailey punched the two boys repeatedly and was sent to the principal's office by Mrs. Judy Cohen.

Now Bailey was wondering why his mom and dad has invited his former teacher to dinner at the Green family house.

Truthfully, ever since Bailey learned Mrs. Cohen was coming to dinner tonight, he kept thinking to himself over and over about why Mrs. Cohen is coming over for dinner.

His mind was thinking to himself; why is it Mrs. Cohen is coming to dinner at his home?

He knows he's been getting good grades at school, has never gotten himself into trouble, and as of a matter of fact, the last time he ever visited the school principal's office was when the incident happened.

After the punching incident, Bailey was forever the role model student.

At least Bailey thought so!

Now Bailey just doesn't know what to do, and is very nervous.

Especially when Mom told Bailey to put his blue suit on with a shirt with a tie – Bailey was so nervous.

Oh boy - this is getting very serious.

My stomach is queasy.

Bailey is feeling awful.

He keeps thinking to himself, what did I do!

Just as Bailey was sitting at the kitchen table and was about to ponder what to do, Brandon walked into the kitchen.

Brandon greeted him, "Hi Bailey."

Bailey replied, "Hi yourself."

Brandon asked Bailey, "Is something troubling you?"

Bailey replied, "Absolutely Brandon - I'm a good person and you really like me as your little brother, don't you?"

Brandon was looking at Bailey and replied jokingly, "Well, let me think." Brandon continued to jokingly say, "Maybe, maybe not! What do you think Bailey? Of course, you are my best buddy and special brother. Yes, I think you are a very awesome brother – why do you ask! Did something happen?"

Bailey replied, "You do know that my former math teacher, Mrs. Cohen, is coming to dinner?"

Brandon replied, "Yeah – mom told me - is something wrong?"

Bailey told Brandon, "You know why she is coming to dinner!"

Brandon replied, "I don't know actually – am I missing something?"

Bailey replied, "Well, you do remember, the incident!"

Brandon acting dumb, "What incident, I do not know, did something happen in the past?"

Bailey replied, "You know, the punching."

Brandon acting dumb again, "What punching, what that awful thing you did in Mrs. Cohen's classroom?"

Bailey was so exasperated by this time – "Okay Brandon, I really would like to know. Am I in trouble from Mom and Dad? Why is Mrs. Judy Cohen coming to dinner at our house?"

Brandon replied, "Oh that…….. I guess Mrs. Cohen came to Dad's hardware store yesterday to buy some stuff, and Dad thought it would be nice to invite Mrs. Judy Cohen, since she was and still is your favorite teacher."

Bailey was relieved, and sighed, "Oh thank goodness, I thought maybe I was in for big trouble. Thanks Brandon for telling me the reason why Mrs. Cohen is coming to our house for dinner. What a relief. You have no idea how nervous I was all morning – ever since Mom told me."

Brandon was hugging Bailey, "Everything will be fine. Besides, now you get to wear your new blue suit tonight."

Bailey replied, "Yes indeed."

# Chapter 4

## Brandon and Pedro

It was late Saturday mid-morning and Brandon was just about to finish his piano music theory book and math homework. Bailey knocked on his room door, and told him, "Your friend, Pedro, the hockey nut-so guy, is here."

As Pedro was walking inside Brandon's room, Pedro starts talking, "Wow! Hey, Brandon, you really do have a lot of books! Do you ever get tired of reading them?"

Brandon replied, "No Pedro – I enjoy listening to classical piano music and reading all the literature books. The other books I read sometimes, but it's not like reading the literature books."

Pedro replied, "Brandon, you never take yourself too seriously. That is one thing I do really like about you. You are never brash or stuck up. You are taught to have great humbleness, honesty, integrity, and humility.  That is what my Dad always tells me about you, Brandon.  Did you know that my Dad really, oh oh really, likes you?  If you only knew how highly my Dad thinks of you.  My Dad always tells me to hang out with you a lot!"

Brandon really did not know how to respond to this statement.  He responded by saying, "Gee, Pedro, thank you very much.  I'm very much humbled."  Pedro replied, "See how humble you are Brandon.  You are very much welcome!"

As that conversation was winding down, Pedro was in deep thoughts as to how to ask Brandon his next questions.

Brandon asked Pedro, "Earth to Pedro, you look like someone who has a lot on his mind - is there trouble Pedro?"  Pedro replied, "Ohhh………. not, not, not really.  It is just that how, how, how, how, how you are so wise beyond your age!  I wish I could be like you in the sense that I could be very wise."

Brandon had a big smile and looked at his good friend Pedro fondly with a big smile on his face, **"Listen Pedro, you are you!**

**I Brandon am Brandon!**

## Bailey is Bailey!

Don't try to emulate me or my brother David. You have to be who you are. Remember David Green is the hockey guy. I, Brandon, remember when David was young, and how disciplined and hard-working he was. He worked very, very, very hard to become a professional hockey player. You would not believe how laser-sharp-focused David was. Most of all, my older brother, David, is very honest, with good integrity, and is trying to be the best in his field."

Brandon continued, "David would always tell me: Brandon work hard, and do not get yourself into trouble.

David would always give me advice as he was a very philosophical guy."

Brandon continued to have a conversation as he was observing Pedro looking around his room and was proceeding to open the book cover of one of his Mozart piano books.

"When you are going through trials, it's difficult to think of yourself as blessed. But you know what! You have so much in your life now and you have so many good things coming."

Pedro replies, "Yes, you're right, Brandon, many good things will be coming my way."

Brandon says, "Listen Pedro: some people are going to hurt you **(of course not me, Pedro! Because I am your best friend)**, they will do unfair things, abandon you when you need them the most and probably say very hurtful things, but you can let it go. You are too blessed to worry about the people who say hurtful things to you, don't worry."

Pedro replied, "Yes, Brandon, you are my best friend. Therefore, I don't need to worry about you doing unfair things to me."

Brandon said, "You're correct. On another note, when you have faith, faith is too good. You just go and smile and enjoy this daily. Yes, you may have to fight and argue, but remember most of the time you can just let it go. You don't need to hold a grudge. You can accept people just as who they are. Nobody's perfect," he said to Pedro.

Brandon continued to talk:

"Think of the joyful things you do have in your life right now, and be resilient.

I want to expand on that thought further and share with you that criticism is part of achievement.

If you are achieving anything, prepare to be betrayed, offended, and slandered.

It will happen and it is a natural part of leading and influencing others. You want to do great things with your life! Prepare to be gossiped and lied about and also put down. You need to have the ability to lead with an equal tolerance for pain. You can't sit around being offended all day or being worried about what people say about you.

If you believe in yourself and have faith, you can do anything you put your mind to. It will help you to experience and to strengthen your positive attitude and your leadership skills."

Pedro said, "You think I have leadership skills, Brandon?"

Brandon said, "Of course you do - everybody has leadership skills if you put your mind to it. You need to be resilient!"

Pedro, "Oh, you think I could have a mindset of being resilient?"

Brandon, "Yes, you most definitely could do that. Some people are offensive and always will be. The only thing you can do is to be resilient. Don't be the kind of person who hinges on praise and criticism."

Pedro says, "I like the praise but don't care for the criticism."

Brandon says, "You have to have both. You can't always find what you are looking for. There is always good and bad to everything."

Pedro said, "See, that is why my Dad says you are the most wonderful student in the whole wide world. That is why my Dad tells me to hang around with you a lot. He thinks I could learn a lot of wisdom from you, which does happen. I am very grateful that you are my very best friend."

Brandon says, "Yes, Pedro. Thank you very much for the compliment. I am proud to be your best friend."

Brandon was looking at Pedro, thinking how he could continue to say what was on his mind. He decided to tell Pedro what he was thinking.

Brandon said, "Listen Pedro. Always listen like a wise owl. Wisdom can come from positive, sound-minded people."

"Wow, Brandon! Cool and awesome," said Pedro excitedly to Brandon.

Brandon was looking at Pedro and decided to stand up, ready to go downstairs to the kitchen, looking forward to having milk and cookies.

"OK Pedro, that is enough talk. Let's go downstairs to have milk and cookies. Don't let other students tell you what to do," said Brandon.

Pedro put his arms around Brandon's shoulder, "You see why when I am in a down mood you always inspire me to be the person I want to be. I really thank you for this talk we had today. You know what, your brother Bailey is one hundred percent correct. I am a hockey-nutso guy from Spain."

# Chapter 5

## Brandon's Piano Trouble

When you believe in something the impossible becomes possible!

My name is Brandon Green, and I am totally into playing classical piano music.

I am always dreaming of being on stage, performing piano music with a full one hundred, grand scale, orchestra, and I do have dreams of conducting in the most awesome, really great and beautiful, famous concert halls.

My passions and goals in life are to play the piano in both Carnegie Hall and Royal Albert Hall. These goals are in addition to the goal of becoming a conductor.

Okay.

Those are my goals!

One day, Brandon was in his room and was looking out the window for a little bit of time, truly admiring the tranquil-ness of Lake Swan and the beauty of the green marsh.

He was thinking to himself before he saw a picture of him and Bailey smiling together on a picture frame on top of his desk.

He then began to scan over the many, many, many trophies he had won over several years.

Brandon was thinking to himself during this time – is it ever going to happen?  Maybe he, Brandon, could really become a concert piano artist and perhaps become an orchestra conductor!

Yes,

One of my goals is to become a concert pianist.

This past year, it seems that I, Brandon, was not really focused or driven to win, nor did I have the will to win.  It was simply not there.

I have found out that I really am not having extra motivation like my older brother David, who was, and is I mean totally obsessed on becoming a true NHL hockey player.   For me, maybe because I have become complacent playing the piano or something else, I, Brandon, have not quite figured it out yet.

The good news is that I, Brandon, am still determined and am resolute to become a concert piano artist.

I miss my previous piano teacher, whose name was Mrs. Lucille Ospena. She was the one who always used to say to me, "Now Brandon, you must always practice, practice, and practice."

Brandon Green, the piano guy, or maybe not!

Ever since I was five years old, I knew what I wanted to do when I grew up.

I thought I did!

As you guessed, it was playing classical piano music.

I, Brandon, would dream of being on a stage, performing on a nine-foot grand piano for the sold-out performance inside the concert hall.

I would dream of ever so gently and lightly and airily touching the beautiful black and white ivory keys to bring out the most awesome – eloquently beautiful melody and sound acoustics of classical piano music.

One afternoon, Brandon was practicing piano, and was thinking to himself and reminiscing how Mrs. Lucille Ospena thought it would be good for Brandon to learn more technique, even though Brandon thought he could play Bach's piano work "The Well-Tempered Clavier." As it was, Mrs. Ospena was right. I needed to improve my piano technique before playing the piece well.

I do miss Mrs. Ospena very much.

At the beginning it was very awkward, she being my elementary school teacher then as my piano teacher.

I thought it was bad enough that I saw Mrs. Ospena every day at school for at least one hour then on top of that I had to see her again sometime during the weekend for three hours.

I did feel like I did see her wayyyyyyyy more than I would like it to be so.

I felt this way even though I was always excited and looking forward to going to piano – piano - piano lessons at her quaint little white cottage.

Mrs. Lucille Ospena was very much an eccentric music teacher.

I, Brandon, could still visualize her quaint little white cottage on Swan Lake.

When I first opened her front door, you would immediately see the two black lacquer, shiny, seven-foot Steinway pianos side by side and one flowery sofa.

Her house was very cluttered with old antiques and baskets were scattered everywhere.

Then, many years later, I learned that Mrs. Ospena was moving and would no longer be teaching piano lessons to me. It was the saddest day for me.

Mrs. Lucille Ospena's last parting words to me were, as you have guessed!

Practice, practice, practice, and do it again!

I'm forever thankful that I, Brandon, did have a wonderful music teacher like Mrs. Lucille Ospena.

# Chapter 6

## Brandon's Tree

The tiny bungalows dotted the front of Lake Swan, once a former home to Mrs. Lucille Ospena.

My former piano teacher's home has gone through major renovations.

I remember when I first walked into this quaint little cottage, which I spent time in, from when the Green family first moved to this little peaceful, tranquil little county town overlooking Lake Swan with a population of 3,500.

Springdale is a rural community in the northeastern corner of the state of Minnesota. The town is very small, rural, and has a quaint, folksy atmosphere.

Oh yes, Mrs. Ospena's lifestyle is more eccentric than my Grandma Ruth's lifestyle. Mrs. Ospena's house is about fifteen miles from my house. Her little tiny bungalow is a tiny one-bedroom white cedar-shingled house that had no heater for the winter.

When I first opened her front door on the first day of my piano lesson, the immediate thing you saw was her quaint living room containing two seven-foot Steinway black, shiny, lacquer pianos side-by-side and one sofa.

I remember how in addition to the Steinway pianos it was cluttered with very unique, old antiques and there were baskets everywhere.

Mrs. Ospena told Grandma Ruth that I, Brandon, was the first very talented student she had in her piano music studio in the past fifteen years.

I remember very fondly how Mrs. Ospena often told me, "Striving for the best will bring you closer to the best."

When I first won a major piano competition, Mrs. Ospena was so very excited - she suggested that we, Brandon and Mrs. Ospena, plant a tree together outside her house to celebrate together. Mrs. Ospena treated this as a special occasion.

I remember asking Mrs. Ospena, "Why plant a tree?"

Her reply to me was, "It's a great symbol for Brandon. It reminds you that you are you, Brandon! You'll be reminded of this particular win."

This past spring, Mr. Wonjiskie decided to renovate the tiny little bungalow cottage to add a heater and update the looks.

Brandon was thinking to himself - he hoped that Mr. Wonjiskie would not take out the "tree" that he and Mrs. Ospena planted together.

Much to his delight, Mr. Wonjiskie assured Brandon that "the tree will not be replaced." Mr. Wonjiskie grew up in a town near the Vistula River in Poland, and told Brandon that when he first saw a tumble-down Lake Swan cottage it was the most divine memory of childhood.

"It was the rockaways all over again." As I walked in, I could feel my childhood - spending time with my grandparents. Therefore, I understand the sentimental value you, Brandon, have with the "tree" you and Mrs. Ospena planted together.

"The place really warms my heart."

Built about forty years ago, the cedar-shingled house had no heater installed or insulation.

He was in for a little surprise.  It turned out Springdale's regulations required Mr. Wonjiskie to bring everything else up to code.  He found himself rebuilding the house, installing a new roof, new walls, new floors, and new ceilings.  Mr. Wonjiskie said, "My little renovation turned out to be a huge project."  Despite some major changes, Mr. Wonjiskie said he did his best to keep the little cottage in the spirit of the place.  Mr. Wonjiskie kept the inside of the home's living room like that of Mrs. Ospena's living room minus all the antique basket collections.

The home's former interior had dark wood that made it resemble a sailboat house.  He replaced it, giving it walls that had bright blue and white stripes and cherry-wood floors.

The previous owner, Mrs. Lucille Ospena, had owned the little cottage house for forty years.  For part of the time, Mrs. Ospena was a painter when she was not working.  Mr. Wonjiskie kept most of Mrs. Ospena's painted pictures of nautical scenes that were throughout the home and re-distributed them within the house.  A cupboard door painted with sailboats was moved from the kitchen to one of the piano room walls.  A whaling scene in the bathroom now hangs in a hallway.  Mr.

Wonjiskie salvaged a piece of wood where Mrs. Ospena's piano students engraved signatures. Mr. Wonjiskie said, "It's hung like art."

One thing Mr. Wonjiskie liked was a palette of white, blue, and gray on the sofa. He also liked this kind of palette on the two chairs. Mr. Wonjiskie said he acknowledged that when his piano students come in, the spills would likely occur; therefore, he chose very sturdy, spill-resistant fabric for the furniture. Like I've said before, "A bunch of kids in the house is always something I like." With the renovation complete, Mr. Wonjiskie said, "It's my little gateway to music heaven."

Even with all the construction, Brandon was quite pleased that his personal, sentimental tree that he planted with Mrs. Ospena had endured and had thrived. The tree still lives! And I'm so happy that Mr. Wonjiskie did everything he could to save Brandon's sentimental tree.

# Chapter 7

## Grandma Ruth

Serene beauty!

Some people take the easy path, but my Grandma Ruth never took the easy path in her life.

This crispy morning, as Grandma Ruth was sitting on the front porch, she was admiring and how beautiful Lake Swan was - how it was serene and peaceful. Grandma Ruth was enjoying the scenery in front of her.

Grandma Ruth was fondly looking at Brandon as Brandon came out of the house.

Brandon greeted Grandma Ruth, "How about I sit next to you, Grandma?"

Grandma Ruth said, "Certainly you're welcome to do so, I would be delighted."

Brandon said, "Thank you, Grandma Ruth."

Grandma Ruth said, "You're very welcome. We can have a little chat together."

Brandon asked Grandma Ruth, "Ever since you, Grandma Ruth, first moved in with us, the Green family, I've observed you over time and I've decided to ask some questions. They have been on my mind, but I have always chickened out."

Then Grandma Ruth said, "Ask me away, whatever it is. Don't be a chicken."

Brandon smiled, and looked at Grandma, "Can I ask you something?"

Grandma Ruth replied, "Okay, yes Brandon. Hopefully, it is not too complicated of a question."

Brandon replied, "No, it will not be a complicated question. I'm not good at doing those kinds of things."

Then Grandma Ruth replied, "Good."

Brandon asked Grandma Ruth, "Are you really glad and happy that you moved in with us?"

Grandma Ruth was somewhat surprised, but answered Brandon without looking at him, "Indeed, I'm very happy and most definitely glad that I've made my own luck."

Brandon replied, "Your own luck?"

Grandma Ruth said, "I most certainly took advantage of circumstances, sometimes simply being at the right place, at the right time!"

Brandon replied, "So you made your own luck for yourself?  What do you mean by sometimes simply being at the right place at the right time?"

Grandma Ruth replied, "Yes I made my own luck.  I guess you can say I took advantage of the situation and made my own luck."

Brandon replied, "What do you mean took advantage and made your own luck?"

Grandma Ruth replied, "Yes, that's what I did.  I made luck for myself."

"So you took advantage of we the Green family and made luck for yourself?"  Brandon jokingly told that to his grandma.

Then Grandma Ruth replied, with a smile on her face, "Yes I did something like that."

Brandon replied, "Boy I would have never thought my Grandma Ruth would be a very shrewd person."

Grandma Ruth replied, "I'm not a shrewd person. I just took advantage of the moment that was there for me."

Brandon said, "Wow, Grandma Ruth, I would never have thought you would be that kind of person, a shrewd person." Brandon said this jokingly.

Grandma Ruth replied, "Well I don't exactly call myself a shrewd person, but I do know when luck is on my side; and I grabbed the opportunity with your family and was able to move in afterwards!"

Brandon replied, "Well, Grandma Ruth, you made luck for yourself."

Grandma Ruth said, "Yes I did. I made luck for myself."

Brandon replied, "Yes, indeed, Grandma Ruth. You really made a good luck choice for yourself."

Grandma Ruth told Brandon, "Oh no, I think you are mis-reading my statement, Brandon."

Then Brandon said, "How is it that I'm misreading your statement Grandma Ruth, if you don't mind my asking?"

Grandma Ruth replied, "My luck occurred at the intersection of random chance. The good news is that, in life in general, if you look, there is plenty of luck to go around. You have to know when and how to look for it."

Brandon replied, with a quizzical look on his face, facing toward his Grandma Ruth, "Like meeting Grandpa Chester? There was luck in meeting Grandpa Chester!"

Grandma Ruth said, "Yes indeed. Did you know that your Grandpa Chester was one of the humblest people I have ever known?"

Brandon replied, "Oh, so Grandpa Chester was a very humble person?"

Grandma Ruth said, "Yes, indeed. Besides being humble, your Grandpa Chester was a very loyal person and a loyal friend to everyone he ever met."

Brandon says, "It seems like he was a very nice man!"

Grandma Ruth said, "I was a big fan of Grandpa Chester. He was an extremely competitive and positive person."

Brandon asked, "Oh, yes, I remember that when you had your accident, you could not be a ballet dancer anymore. Grandpa Chester was interviewing you, if I recall?"

Grandma Ruth replied, "Yes, that's true. Did you know when he first met me in the hospital, I was all feeling sorry for myself. He brought me a yellow and pink bouquet of flowers to cheer me up. He was hilarious - he did not know a thing about ballet."

Brandon said, "That must have been a very interesting interview he had with you!"

"Yes, it was. I knew he was going to visit me the next day. I purchased a book for your Grandpa about how to become a ballet dancer," Grandma Ruth said this as she was looking at Lake Swan.

Brandon replied, "Do you think Grandpa read the book?"

Grandma Ruth replied, with a big smile on her face, "Yes he did - maybe because he really wanted to make me smile and laugh. He was genuinely kind and caring. He was the greatest friend to everyone."

Brandon told Grandma Ruth, "Thank you very much for the conversation. Sometimes you have to let go of the picture of what you thought life would be like and learn to find joy in the story you are actually living."

Grandma Ruth was very fond of her grandson Brandon, and loved sharing stories with him. "I am the luckiest person, and how great is that!  I have this golden opportunity to live with Brandon, Bailey, David, and their Mom and Dad."

# Chapter 8

# Random Acts of Kindness

Living Water

If you have ever experienced a long-term drought, you understand how essential water is.

Plants dry up, crops fail, and before long the ground cracks and dust starts to blow.  Sometimes, this is how life feels too – dry, fruitless, unsatisfying, and futile.

If you have faith and are a believer, the external impacts from your life resemble a drought, but inside you have the ever-flowing living water of faith.

Life is like a continually moving stream.  We are comforted when we experience the light.  We find solace and comfort when we are hurting.  We all need to find inner peace and to have convictions that guide our lives.  We can be cleansed with living water, something that always prompts and keeps you from heading down the wrong path.

We all need to not live a dry, fruitless life.

The more we learn to have faith in our walk of life, the more living water will flow through us.

These are the thoughts of minister Patrick Cerrium.

Three days a week our church, the Springdale Presbyterian Church, has a community outreach program. This service provides a hot home-cooked meal on Monday, Wednesday, and Thursday nights for people needing extra help.

The Green family has been volunteering at the community outreach program for the past several years. It has been run by the local church minister Patrick Cerrium for over twenty years.

A total of ten families now volunteer.

"It appears that a lot less families are coming to the hot meal service this year so far compared to the past!

I do hope folks have found good jobs.

Wherever those folks who are not coming are, let's hope that they are doing well and send well wishes to them all," said Minister Patrick Cerrium to John Green.

Reverend Cerrium was telling John Green: "Many people are having difficult family relationships. Especially alcoholism and drugs are really at the center of many of their personal struggles and therefore affecting all of their personal lives and their families," said Reverend Cerrium.

Minister Cerrium is a man of great compassion and kindness, and shows reverence to all people who need help.

In his younger days, he was hoping to become a professional basketball player. He has never been married, is tall and very thin, wears very thick glasses, and is a very generous and humble, and is a kind-hearted, caring man.

As the minister was standing next to John Green, and was serving hot meals, he was telling John Green that more and more people will be struggling to pay their winter home heating bills each month during the winter months.

A lot of families have to choose either the food on the table or paying the harsh winter electric bills in the winter months. Reverend Cerrium was telling John Green, "Have you heard that Mr. Louis Wonjiskie is having a little bit of a tough time during these last several months?"

John Green was very surprised, and looked at Reverend and asked: what tough times?

"It is very apparent we cannot have this conversation here on this sensitive subject. Why don't you come by my house tomorrow morning and we might continue this conversation?" said John Green.

Early the next morning, Reverend Cerrium was at our Green family house before 8:00 a.m. very much anxious to talk with John Green.

John Green asked Reverend Cerrium, "What is this — what tough times are happening for Mr. Louis Wonjiskie?"

Reverend Cerrium replied, "As you know, the last year and a half, he has been re-modeling his little cottage. It turned out that he has encountered a lot more trouble from the Springdale building code department as well as extra unforeseeable problems and extra expenses."

John Green replied, "Hmmm…. I see."

Reverend Cerrium continues, "Before he began the project, he budgeted a large sum for the project. In the end, he spent roughly twice that amount, including plans, installation for heating, designer fees, architect fees; he had to re-grade his driveway, re-do his lighting, spend money on furniture, contractors' fees, and pay for materials, labor, and structural changes."

John Green replied, "Yes I actually do remember hearing something about how the house had no heater or insulation. Also, Springdale's regulations required Mr. Wonjiskie to bring everything else up to code. It is very sad that Mr. Wonjiskie had other unforeseeable problems."

Reverend Cerrium replied, "Yes, poor dear man!"

John Green replied, "How unfortunate that it seems like he is practically building a brand-new house!"

Reverend Cerrium was clearing his throat, not knowing how to mention his next question, "Ah, yes, John Green, isn't your son, Brandon, taking piano lessons from Louis? I'm told your son is very fond of him."

John Green replied, "Yes, they both seem to get along very well together."

Reverend Cerrium tells John Green, "Look here, John, I'm here this morning to ask you a big favor. As I have told you earlier, Louis has encountered extra, extra, extra expenses which he was not expecting that are overwhelming. Also, on top it all – that poor man also encountered bad luck when his investment advisor swindled most of his money and took off. Now, he is having an extraordinarily tough time paying his utility bills."

By this time, John Green was watching the Reverend's face very seriously and intensely and said, "So, Reverend, you're here this morning to do what?" John Green was smiling at Reverend Cerrium.

Reverend Cerrium replied quickly, "Yes, indeed, amen! You're going to help Louis out!"

Reverend Cerrium continued, "Again, I would like to say this from the bottom of my heart, may God bless you and the Green family."

John Green was so shocked by what he had just heard from the Reverend. The only thing he could think of was, "Thank you very much Reverend Cerrium."

Minister Cerrium told John Green, "I knew you would help Louis - thank you and God bless you."

# Chapter 9

## Contest

# Whoooooooooo……….

Snow – snow – snow – snow – snowing!

Never ending snow.

It kept on snowing for two solid whole weeks, non-stop.

Yes, we live in the snow country of Springdale, Minnesota.

We are to be expecting tons of snow in the months of:

January, February, March, April

Sometimes May, and then maybe June.

But in October?

It is totally a white-out-snow storm!

We have so much snow.  It is a total white out.

My Grandma Ruth, mom, and dad jokingly said, "We need to build a tunnel to get around the town."

Snow is covering everything!

I just can't believe we are having a major snowstorm, and it's October.

Guess what?

This year, we have, what you could say, an early Halloween surprise.

None – of – us – kids could go out on Halloween – we couldn't trick or treat again.

No such luck this year again!

My little brother, Bailey, was so much looking forward to Halloween night.

You see, Bailey had been pondering and thinking of this year's Halloween costume for several months.

This year, he was to be a computer-key board.

What a disappointment!

Poor Bailey, he really wanted to show off his new Halloween costume which our mom and Grandma Ruth had home-made for Bailey.

Snow is covering everything.

I just can't believe this kind of October snow is happening!

No joke, no kidding.

Most of all, we finally have no school for one whole week.

Snow week!

Snow is everywhere.

Totally white out!

Snow is covering everything.

Since it is snowing so much, Grandma Ruth suggested to Bailey and Brandon that we should go outside and have a snowman building contest.

First, we all have to put on our heavy jackets, boots, scarfs, hats, mittens, and earmuffs. It was snowing very heavily, but the snow is wet and sticks together.

Bailey makes his snowman.

Grandma Ruth makes her snowman.

Brandon makes his snowman.

Well, the snowman building contest was not as easy as it appeared to be. Grandma Ruth was certainly a shoo-in for the win before the contest began.

Bailey's snowman consists of only two balls, one big ball, and one small ball at the top.

Grandma Ruth's snowman consists of two medium balls on top of each other and one small ball on top.

Brandon's snowman consists of the big bottom ball, a medium ball, and a small ball on top to distinguish the snowman.

We all used carrot sticks for the nose, black charcoal for the eyes, and three small black golf balls to make a smile. Grandma Ruth's snowman contains extra fashion; it has a red hat on top of the snowman, and Bailey's snowman and Brandon's snowman have black hats on top of each snowman.

Grandma Ruth and Bailey both agree that, "I, Brandon, have won the snowman building contest." Brandon was most certainly confident of the win with this statement.

Later, just as we all were ready to go back inside the warm house and were looking forward to drinking hot cocoa, Bailey heard someone shouting his name from far away.

Brandon realized it was Sara, Kelly Chin's younger sister, who was calling Bailey.

Soon, Bailey, Brandon, Kelly, and Sara were having a fun snow day together.

Even Grandma Ruth joined the snowball throwing.

After having a fun time with snowball throwing, Grandma Ruth said, "Making the snowman and participating in the snowman building contest was fun."

Bailey replied, "Yes, it was really fun. It's just that I did not win the contest!"

Brandon, Kelly, and Sara replied, all in unison, "Maybe next time."

Finally, it was getting late. Therefore, Sara, Kelly, Grandma Ruth, Bailey, and Brandon – all of them decided to go back inside the warm house and enjoy the hot cocoa together, as it was snowing heavily outside.

Fun day!

# Chapter 10

## Who Is This Pug?

Who is this pug?

Mr. Applebee has been a neighbor of the Green family for the last several years.  He is very much an eccentric old man.  In the past, no one in town seemed to know too much about Mr. Stuart Applebee.

He also very much lives somewhat of a hermit lifestyle.

In the past several years, the rumor was really flying around that he used to be a very famous soccer player under a pseudonym and etc. – etc. – etc.!

**Well, guess what!**

Mr. Applebee, who now lives a hermit lifestyle, was a very famous Formula One Racing Car Driver!

Indeed, as it turned out, Mr. Stuart Applebee was a world-famous Formula One race car driver. Mr. Applebee did not play soccer or rugby, as some rumors had either one as the answer to the question of what did Mr. Applebee do for a living in the past.

How awesome it is that he was a Formula One race car driver!

Here we go again!

My little brother, Bailey, was sitting on the front porch steps and was thinking to himself - he wished Pepper was still here.

You see, Pepper was Mr. Applebee's previous Golden Labrador.

Bailey and Pepper always liked to play near the marsh of Lake Swan.

Almost daily, Bailey also played in front of the porch in front of our house with Pepper.

Somehow my little brother, Bailey, was very fond of Mr. Applebee and his dog named Pepper.

Most of the time after school, Bailey and Pepper would play with each other with Bailey throwing a wooden stick for Pepper to retrieve.

Every time Bailey tossed the wooden stick out onto the meadow field, Pepper bounded after it, brought it back, and dropped it at Bailey's feet.

Pepper would then wag his tail proudly and wait for Bailey to throw the stick again.

Bailey always decided that Mr. Applebee's dog was very, very, very smart, intelligent, and was the most awesome dog to ever fetch sticks from Bailey. Bailey would teach Pepper to do something useful.

One day, he even tossed Pepper a bundle of newspaper out onto the marsh field; Pepper would run super-fast after bounding after it, bring it back, and drop the bound newspaper at Bailey's feet.

Pepper would then wag his tail proudly and wait for Bailey to throw the bound bundle of newspaper again. When Pepper would drop the paper at Bailey's feet, Bailey would pat Pepper, and say, "What a good dog, Pepper, you are the smartest dog ever Pepper!"

Pepper would then wiggle and wag his tail with happiness and delight.

Often times, at the sight of the wooden stick, Pepper would spring to his feet.

Pepper would, "Woof… Woof…. Woof… Woof… Woof" and wag his tail.

Yesterday afternoon, when Bailey was sitting in front of our house porch and thinking about Pepper, Bailey noticed this small dog with distinctive features of a wrinkly, short-muzzled face, and a curled tail that was barking and barking at Bailey.

It was very obvious that this little dog was being very sociable and wanted to play with Bailey.

Without any thoughts, Bailey threw a bundle of newspaper he was holding - he decided to throw it out and see what this little guy – the dog – would do.

Well guess what!

This little dog with a short-muzzled face ran super-fast and chased after the bundle - going after it - and brought it back to Bailey, dropping it at Bailey's feet.

Then, this little dog would wag his tail and hope that Bailey would throw the bundle of newspaper again.

Bailey told this little cute dog that you are a smart, an incredibly smart dog. He told this little dog, "I used to play with Mr. Applebee's very smart dog named Pepper."

# Chapter 11

## David Green - "The Cup"

### The Stanley Cup Competition

First, the good news.

The Colorado Blue Birds have reached the Stanley Cup finals on the strength of their speed, skill, and their ability to operate at a fast tempo - and the depth that allowed them to roll four lines.

Emphasizing speed and youth are growing trends in the National Hockey League. The Colorado Blue Birds have added several young players to possibly hoist the NHL's ultimate prize -

The Stanley Cup.

Other teams will try to replicate the Blue Birds' move related to the playing of the season by establishing a brisk pace and asking swift-skating youth to lead them.

There will be moments of pure skill and brilliance and moments when that speed produces cringe-worthy defensive mistakes, but the philosophical shift should be entertaining and it certainly should hasten the emergence of the next generation of super-stars.

The continuing presence of speed and skilled players, like David Green, helped to score more goals per game than last season and helped lead the team to accrue more than 100 points.

David is always ready, right from the get-go, because David is prepared to score goals and play the game the right way.

David is always obsessed with three things:

1) What can I do to be a better National Hockey League player, today and tomorrow?

2) What can I do to keep improving tomorrow's game?

3) Lastly, winning the National Hockey League's most coveted prize – the Lord Stanley's Cup.

You see, ever since David was five years old, my big brother was obsessed with playing professional hockey.

Even though my father did not approve of David being a professional hockey player in the future, David figured he had the personal will and determination; and most of all, he very much believed in himself to make it to the National Hockey League.

Today, David plays in the National Hockey League for the Colorado Blue Birds.

He won the ultimate award.

<u>The Stanley Cup</u>

Can the Colorado Blue Birds repeat as champions?

Let's hope so!

David believes it can happen!

Our whole family is evermore proud of David Green's success.

David beat the odds of making it to the National Hockey League.

John Green always wanted David to follow his footsteps of becoming a lawyer and become a lawyer himself instead of a hockey player, but nowadays our father is the biggest fan of David Green.

Now David is the Stanley Cup winner!

Wahoo – Wahoo…………………………..!

W-A-A-H-O-O!    W-A-H-O-O!!

# Chapter 12

## A Leap of Faith

It has been many years since we, the Green family, moved to Springdale, Minnesota, from New York City, New York.

Our lives have truly changed for the better and it's going to continue to be awesome.

We enjoy the rural, quiet, tranquil, slow pace of an easy-living lifestyle.

When my little brother, Bailey, was born with Down syndrome; my Mom and Dad began to look for a quieter lifestyle.

Here we are many, many, many years later, living in a cold, but beautiful, quiet, quaint, picturesque scene of Springdale, Minnesota. It overlooks the beautiful Lake Swan and tall green marsh grass.

Now my parents, John and Megan Green, are the proud owners of the Green hardware store and the supermarket.

Sometimes, the unexpected things happen.

"Who would have thought that John and Megan Green, my parents, would have purchased and become the owners of the hardware store and a super market in a small, rural town during our family lifetime. My Mom and Dad always remind Bailey and me, Brandon, appreciate what you have! We have a good family." Brandon said this out loud one day.

My dad, John Green, is a very tall, lanky man who has a very imposing figure. He is folksy, friendly, genuine, compassionate, and is a kind-hearted man.

He used to be the general counsel for Goldman Sachs Bank in New York City, New York. He was a hotshot attorney. Being the in-house attorney for an investment banking firm like Goldman Sachs was hard work and often times was very stressful.

My Dad is a person of good character and had excellent skills with regards to his job. My father very much enjoyed his job.

My Mom, Megan Green, is a stay-at-home mom who takes care of the Green family. She always has the sunny outlook. My mom has light brown hair with blue eyes.

Since moving to Springdale, my mother has worked as a part-time receptionist at a local orthodontist office for Dr. Sam Berke. This makes her a house-mom who works as well.

One day, on an early foggy morning, Megan Green was holding a coffee mug on the front porch; looking at and admiring the peaceful, beautiful, and tranquil views of Lake Swan and the green marsh.

Megan Green was reminiscing and thinking to herself, "How lucky can one be in life! Here we are, many years later, in Springdale, Minnesota, living the life of peace and calmness of country living."

Megan Green used to live in New York City, New York, for many, many years. She was not aware that there could be great rewards for living righteously when facing temptations or hardship. We believe we can pursue our dreams and look forward to the life to come, with good conscience. This is what Megan Green believed.

Often times, we go through anguish and pain which are unavoidable in our life; but we can take heart because much spiritual growth happens in adversity.  That is why we hang in there to receive the crown of life when we follow through with blessings and a joyful attitude.

We will be rewarded.  Everything good and right comes to us through living the blessed and joyful life.

Brandon opens the front door, comes outside, and greets his mother, saying, "Hi mom."  Megan Green replied saying, "Hello there, Brandon, have a seat."

Megan Green told Brandon, "I was just reminiscing about how we, the Green family, had moved from New York City, New York, to Springdale, Minnesota."

Megan continues, "Brandon, sometimes you have to overcome struggles and any fears of failure.  You have to be encouraged as you dive into something so you understand how through God's word you are able to face your obstacles with confidence."

Brandon: "Yes, Mom, we certainly have to do that."

"It isn't what you do for a living, what thoughts you have, or how you handle them.  It is that you have to consider the consequences of poor advice – when facing a challenging situation," Mom said.

Mom continued, "It's only natural to turn to family and friends for help.  We must always be careful to examine advice offered to you.  Even though the counsel is motivated by love and seems sound, it is always better to be seeking wise council.  No human being knows all the unseen factors."

Brandon said, "Yes, we do not know all the unseen factors."

Then Mom replied, "Often times, we forget that God's principles never fail."

"Whatever we sow now, we will reap in the future," Mom said.

Brandon replied, "Yes, we can sow now something such as having the good foundation."

"Brandon, you are very wise for your age.  How did I get to be such a lucky mom to have a smart son like you?" Mom said.

Brandon gave his mother a smile, saying, "I'm very thankful myself for a wonderful family."

Mom went on to say, "When we first moved to Springdale, Minnesota, it was a very uncertain place. There was no guarantee from one day to the next.

Brandon, sometimes life is a ladder.  It could be utterly disastrous if we placed our ladder against the wrong wall and after a lifetime of climbing discover that we had wasted all the years."

"Are you glad and happy to be here in Springdale?" asked Mom.

Brandon replied, excitedly, "Yes."

Mom was looking at Brandon's face and continued to talk, "Brandon, life is not always easy; especially, as it pertains to the small things, the annoyances of daily life that can sometimes cause us to walk in a state of frustration instead of easy rhythms of grace."

Brandon replied, "Yes, Mom, I do know that for sure that life is not always easy."

Mom told Brandon, "We always do the best we can. Forging ahead doesn't mean ignoring people or letting people walk all over you.  We were taught that anger is negative.  Sometimes, we think we have done good work, and have extensive knowledge, but others may say our great accomplishments were worthless."

Mom continued to talk as she was looking at Lake Swan, "If our ladder came crashing down, and we have to start over, ask yourself where have you placed your ladder? There is something you can believe – having faith."

Then Brandon chimes in, "Like we are moving to Springdale, Minnesota, that anger is negative in most circumstances-and the thinking is that we shouldn't stand up for ourselves. The key is how you respond."

Brandon continues, "How you respond to people who have huge egos and are weird……!"

Mom was laughing and looking at Brandon's face, "Well, Brandon, that was something I had not thought of – but there's something about it that allows me to be offended, but to not lash out, and then to give it up."

Megan continued talking, "When you forgive big things, it becomes easier to forgive little things. It enables us to be a more compassionate person daily. The Lord is asking you to forgive, to bless, and to enter into new life, teaching us to bless those who have wronged us in a true spirit of forgiveness."

Megan Green continued to talk and tells Brandon, "No matter what happens, we have to look out for each other. Brandon, I want to tell you, thank you for always looking after Bailey. You truly have been a great big brother to Bailey."

Brandon replied, "Thank you Mom – I do feel Bailey is my special little brother.  I will always be a good brother to Bailey no matter what."

Mom said, "Brandon, do you like having Grandma Ruth living with us?"

Brandon said, "I sure do."

Mom asked, "Brandon, do you think Bailey likes having Grandma Ruth living with us?"

Brandon said, "Yes, he sure does like Grandma Ruth living with us."

Mom asked, "Do you think your Dad likes your Grandma Ruth living with us?"

Brandon said, "Originally my sense was that it was a little awkward.  Now, Dad has become fond of Grandma Ruth living with us."

Mom said, "Brandon, you are very wise for your age.  Always be gracious and kind to others.  We are living a very privileged life.  What you don't know will not hurt you. When you discover life, through your faith in God, believe that we have everything required for living wisely, humbly, and well."

Mom continues to talk and looks at Brandon, "I realize that your Grandma Ruth and I – we both have a lot more in common than we thought."

"The way your Grandma Ruth looks at every detail, our minds work a lot more similarly than what we really might have thought," said Mom.

Brandon said, "How blessed we are to be living here in Springdale, Minnesota."

Mom says, "Yes, and we are also able to give back to the community.  We help those who need help and who are not as blessed as we are."

Brandon Green says, "Yes, the amazing thing is that when you help people who need help, your life is much better. You learn to become generous givers."

Mom said, "How blessed we are."

Brandon said, "Yes, indeed, we are very blessed."

Mom said, "You do know we sacrificed a lot when we uprooted our family to Springdale, Minnesota, several years ago.  Brandon, did you know there is more to life than a job and a prestigious lifestyle?  Make an impact and be a good role model to your little brother, Bailey. David is a good role model for you, Brandon.  Always have a good soul.  Express courage.  A good lifestyle requires that our conversation, conduct, and character reflect that we are walking with God in righteousness."

Brandon was listening to his mother very intently, "Yes, always listen, trust, and obey."

Mom said, "No one is perfect.  We always have to do our best.  Here we are in Springdale, Minnesota, a picturesque, quiet, little rural town full of quietness nearby a beautiful and tranquil Lake Swan, which has a lush marsh surrounding it.  We, as a family, have a wonderfully blessed life in Springdale, Minnesota."

# Have – a – Hoot – Ha – Day!

# About the Author

Kevin graduated from Stanford University with a Bachelors of Science degree in Chemistry. Kevin was a spelling bee winner, advancing to Washington, D.C., in fifth grade, and he also was an award-winning pianist.

His first book was title *Sixth Grade and Growing Up*, and his second book was titled *Green Family: New Home*. His third book is titled *Seventh Grade and Friendship*. His fourth book is *The Green Family: Grateful*. His fifth book is *Eighth Grade and Togetherness*. His sixth book is *The Green Family: Blessings*. His seventh book is *The Hsu Family: Finding Happiness*, and the eight book is *The Green Family: Bailey Being Bailey*. His ninth book is entitled *The Hsu Family: Calvin and Pedro Good Friends*. He is working on a short-story sequel as the next book.

**All the books can be found on Amazon.com.**

Thank you very much for purchasing this book.

Made in the USA
Las Vegas, NV
27 July 2021